FOLLOW YOUR HEART

by

Nancy Holland

For Beth

Nancy Holland
December 2001

ISBN: 0-75965-266-X

This book is printed on acid free paper.

1stBooks – rev. 08/15/01

INTRODUCTION

Memories are as diverse as most other things in life. Most memories are like the fog that creeps in at night, leaving a misty, watercolor haze just above the ground. As the morning appears, the outlines on the trees and houses take on wavy shapes and appear as if in a dream until the sun comes shining through. Then the Florida sky turns it's indigo blue and everything becomes clear and bright.

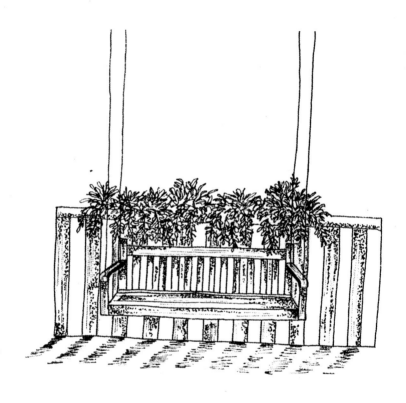

Chapter One

Being an only child for most of my childhood, I spent a lot of time with my mother. I came along in the days when mothers stayed home while the fathers went about the business of making a living for the family. My mother never felt the need to "find herself", she knew who she was and everyone agreed that who she was, was pretty good.

She spent the days before I went to school doing the housework, enjoying the flowers we planted and tended, cooking and making me a part of the small town life that would shape most of the things I was to become. Our time together was a precious thing and looking back on these times I remember so many small, happy things that I will never forget.

My father was the local grocer in our small town of Oak Hill and spent most of his time at the store on Main Street. There was stock to order and put away, customers to serve and accounting to do. He was well respected in the community and his life seemed to be as fulfilling as Mother's was.

We sat on the porch most nights after supper dishes were done and watched the sky turn into night. I remember those days every time I see a sunset. We greeted neighbors as they walked along the sidewalk and sometimes invited them to join us on the porch swing. There were many friends my age to play hopscotch or jump rope with and a game of jacks once

1

in a while. Often after my parents heard my prayers and tucked me in bed I could hear the squeak of the swing as they continued to enjoy the quietness of a small town night and each other. They never talked about their love for each other, but it was obvious to everyone that their's was a marriage to envy. Their love for each other and for me was something I never doubted. They never missed an opportunity to let me know how much they loved me and how blessed we were to be a family. Such was life in the 40's.

As I began my school years time flew by. There were new people in my life and new ways to spend my time. Friendships were made that I treasure still and my horizons went beyond the front porch, but home was still my "haven from the storm" and when things didn't go right at school or with my playmates I knew that there was someplace that I could go and find that things were OK. Life went on much as it always had for our little family as the 40's turned into the 50's and the world changed everywhere else.

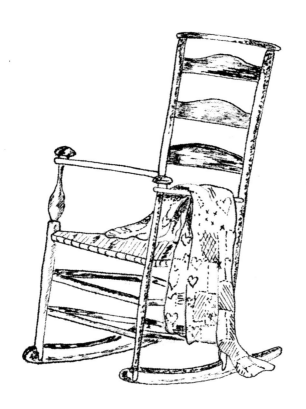

Chapter Two

By the time I was a junior in high school, things changed at home too. My parents told me one night that there would be a new baby in a few months. You can imagine what a shock this was to a teen-age girl. These people were "old", how in the world was a baby conceived between them? Being newly acquainted with the facts of life, I thought I knew all there was to know on the subject of reproduction! I was in a state of shock and dreaded having the whole town know.

My parents were thrilled. Another child to love, as they loved me. It seemed like they were, all of a sudden, younger with so much to look forward to. Soon I too began to look forward to the baby's arrival.

The summer came and we did all the things you do to prepare for a new baby. Mother watched as Father painted the guest room blue. They really wanted a boy. Father and I made a trip up to the dusty attic and brought my old crib down, along with a rocking chair that had been stored there since Grandma died when I was four. It brought back memories of the days she spent with us and I began to realize how memories become a part of our lives. I spent days putting a coat of shiny white enamel on the crib and rocking chair. I was as proud as they were of the outcome of the nursery. Even brought my best friend up to see it. It was hard to imagine what it would be like to share my folks with someone else, but I was ready.

As summer arrived Mother was tired a lot and depended on me to help out with the housework. My two years of home-economics were put to good use as I learned how to keep the laundry done. A wringer washer, two rinse tubs and a clothes line were the "tools of the trade". I soon learned to watch the sky to see if the afternoon rain clouds were close so that the clothes on the line would not get wet again. I sat on the swing and read CHERRY AMES with one eye on the sky most mornings. The clean, sweet smell of the sheets and towels fresh from the sunshine lingers with me still as I fold them from the dryer. No dryer-sheets can really bring that smell back, only memories.

Every afternoon we would work on our "project". Mother had brought out her box of scraps one afternoon soon after school holidays had started and announced that we were going to make quilts. "You will be having babies of your own one day", she said, and suggested that I might like to make a baby quilt while she pieced one for "Bobby", as they baby had been referred to lately. So we picked out the pieces of fabric to make up the quilt tops. One basket held the pieces for mine and one for Mother's. We liked the same pieces so often that we decided to make them alike. What a good time we had as we went through the scraps, remembering this dress or that shirt, an apron was made from this piece or "this was your first Easter dress". This is one of the most vivid memories I have of my mother. One of those crystal clear, like yesterday, memories.

The hours we spent cutting and sewing on the old treadle machine were happy times and the quilts became our special bond. We talked about growing up, having babies and, for the first time, Mother gave me advice about the kind of boys she wanted me to date. "You may fall in love young, like your father and I did," she would say. "So don't waste your time on the boys that you feel uncomfortable with. There are plenty of nice young men you have known all your life, just follow your heart." As we quilted tiny stitches and designs on the little quilts, we put little hearts around the borders, to remind ourselves of the words of advice, mother to daughter, "follow your heart."

The quilt for the baby went in the new nursery and the other in my cedar chest, along with the things I had made through the years as I learned to embroidery and crochet. Things that would be in my very own house some day. I knew somehow that my house would be as full of love as this one. I had never known, nor could imagine, any other way.

Finally the big day came and the baby arrived. Father came to get me at school and told me that our "Bobbie" was a little girl. We went to the hospital, checked on a sleeping Mother and then to the nursery to see for the very first time my sister. What an exciting moment for me. She was so tiny and red. But, something was wrong, she was hooked up to all sorts of monitors and had nurses watching her every minute. I was frightened and began to cry. "What's happening?" I asked Father.

We went outside and sat on a bench under a dogwood tree on the hospital lawn before Father spoke. "The baby has a heart condition", he told me. "We didn't expect it and the doctors are real concerned that she won't make it through the day. "I knew you would want to see her." "Now, we must be brave for your mother and help her get through whatever is in store for our little one." I looked up at the clear blue autumn sky and wondered how the sun could be shining and the clouds so innocently drifting by when our baby was in such peril. Was God watching over her? She was so tiny and frail. I took a deep breath and followed Father inside.

With heavy hearts Father and I went to Mother's room and sat by her bed until she wakened. She was calm as the doctors told us about the heart problems, and all the things they were doing for Bobbie. When they left, we held each other and prayed that the little heart would keep beating and grow stronger and that our new baby would live. We talked about all the things we would do with her as she grew and how we would let her know every day of our love.

Mother asked me to get the quilt from the nursery at home and bring it to her. She held it against her heart and prayed that soon she would wrap her tiny daughter in it and take her home.

Mother came home first and I joined her at the hospital every afternoon after school. We watched through the nursery window as Bobbie hung on to life. I think she knew that we needed her to live and our love kept her alive. "Miracles happen," they say and our baby did survive. She came home after a month and I can still feel the little body as I held her and rocked in Granny's rocker in our "blue" nursery. The quilt carefully wrapped around her and the little hearts reminding me of my love for her. Of course, we didn't care that she was not a boy! We thanked God for the tiny child he had given us to love and care for.

My senior year in high school was filled with all the things that you talk about at reunions, football, band practice, proms, broken hearts at the least little thing, friendships shared that you knew would always be a part of your life. The year flew by and before Bobbie was even walking I graduated.

The summer following graduation I spent a lot of time helping around the house. Mother 's time was taken up with the baby, who would always have to be watched and taken to heart specialist for checkups. Her heart would never be healthy, but she was alive! We took turns with her care, even Father, when he came home from the store, would take her out on the porch and slowly swing. The neighbors got used to seeing the two of them every afternoon and would stop and check up on our little miracle baby. She was truly loved by the whole town.

Summer passed quickly and I went to work with Father in the store in the Fall. When Mother needed me at home I was close by to help. Leaving to live and work somewhere else was never an option. I guess life was so good to me that I didn't notice that Mother was tired most of the time, or that she would go to bed at night instead of sitting with us on the porch, or watching the new television we had bought. Father had always worked hard and seldom talked about his feelings so life just went on and I was much the same as I always had been, surrounded by love, and comfortable with my life.

Bobbie was slow to develop, she wasn't even walking on her first birthday. We watched over her like three old hens and rejoiced at each new thing she learned. We had to be careful that she would not get too tired, too hot, too cold, to excited, etc. I would sit on the floor with her on her little quilt and tell her about the hearts quilted in and laugh about Mother's advice about "follow your heart." She would "walk" her tiny fingers around the border of hearts and say "Follow your heart" until we both would roll over with laughter.

Chapter Three

So far there had not been too many choices for my heart to follow. A few of the boys in my graduation class stayed in town and worked, but most went away to college, or to work in larger towns, so I was sure my heart was safe for awhile.

I would have never guessed in a million years that I would lose my heart so quickly and so completely. It all started one afternoon in Father's store. I was working at the cash register when an old station wagon pulled up outside. Six young men and two girls, not much older than I, came in. They spent a lot of time picking out what they wanted and were talkative and friendly. As they placed their choices on the counter and smiled a friendly smile I asked them if they were passing through. I figured they were on their way to another town or to the beach. They introduced themselves to me. Mary was the prettiest of the two girls and the most outgoing. She told me they were a band and had been hired to perform at a local club out on the highway for a few nights. I couldn't imagine being in a band and traveling around the countryside free as a breeze. I was fascinated by this different lifestyle, having known only the quiet protected one that I lived. I had seen bands on the television. We even had one for our senior prom but they were just kids from the town down the road. I was mesmerized by these strangers.

Father came from the supply room and I introduced Mary to him. To my surprise, he liked her immediately. There was something especially sweet about her and he saw it right away. A typical reaction of the father of girls. After finding out that they had tents to sleep in and were looking for someplace to stay for a few days and not having much luck in our little town, he invited them to camp in our back yard. It was really more like a field than a yard. Several acres with fruit trees and a carpet of soft grass. They talked it over and, after a phone call to Mother to OK it with her, they accepted his invitation.

I was so excited, here was another world represented and I wanted to know all about it.

They set up their tents that afternoon as we watched from a distance. I was a little jealous of the interaction of the young people who were so comfortable with each other. They were invited to share supper with us. I heard my parents say afterwards that they had never know more polite and considerate young people.

The other girl's name was Iris. There had never been anyone named Iris in our family or town for that matter. Her fragile gentle personality was exactly what you would think an "Iris" would be like if it became a person. Iris was married to Donald, the band's drummer.. They shared one of the tents. Mary was single and had a tent to herself, while the other three boys bunked in the third one. At my invitation,

Mary agreed to stay in the house in our guest room so the boys could "spread out" in the two tents.

What an exciting few days we had. We listened every afternoon as they practiced and even went to see them perform one night. Mary was the lead singer and quite good. But the leader of the group who played guitar swept me away from the first "hello".

His name was Kevin, and he was the most handsome boy I had ever seen. Actually he wasn't a boy. He was 25 and though I was only 19 he treated me as an adult, which no one else seemed to do. I started staying awake each night until they returned and planned very carefully to be on the porch swing. I'm sure Kevin saw right through my plot but most nights he joined me. We talked about our lives and families a lot. Of course, he talked about the band. It had been a dream of his since he was young to have his own band and maybe make it to the "big time" someday, records, radio, television...His blue eyes would sparkle when he talked about it.

I mentioned to Mary one day, as we were doing some laundry for the band, that I thought Kevin was really great. I was trying to find out if he had a girlfriend or wife somewhere. She gave me a look that told me she knew what I was thinking and said that Kevin was married to the band. He ate, drank and slept with his music and had big dreams of making it to the top. She thought any girl interested in him should know that the band would always come first.

By that time I had decided that surely Kevin would love me and I could make him forget the band and want a life with me. I couldn't imagine any other life than the one I had lived so far happy and protected, as my Mother had always been. But, if having Kevin meant living a different life, even in a tent, then that was what I would do. I went to sleep each night thinking about being with him every night, not just the short time they were camping on our lawn. I found myself humming the music I heard them practicing while I was walking back and forth to the store to work or dusting the shelves. My head was in the clouds and I loved the feeling.

After a couple of weeks the band moved on but not before I received my first "real" kiss. On the front porch one night Kevin had started telling me some things about his life. His parents were both killed in an automobile crash when he was 12 and he had more or less finished raising himself. An aunt and uncle had taken him in but he didn't feel very close to them. He envied my relationship with my parents and still couldn't believe that we had made them all feel so welcome, being perfect strangers and all. He asked if he could call me sometimes and could I come to see them perform. They had several "gigs" close by in the next few months. I was still starry eyed from the kiss and heartbroken when the station wagon pulled out a few days later but was determined that this was not the end of the story for us.

Mother could see what was happening. She knew my heart so well. We had many long talks and she gave me warnings about expecting too much from the relationship, especially when I told her what Mary had said about the band coming first in Kevin's life.

Kevin called almost every night and twice I borrowed the family car and went to see the band at clubs in neighboring towns. We sat in diners before the shows and I could not believe it when Kevin told me how much he missed me and how special I had become to him in such a short time. He confessed that it scared him too. We agreed to take it slow and keep in touch. If love really was our fate, we would know it. We both knew that marriage was a forever thing and only time would tell. I told him about mine and mother's little saying that had carried us through some rough times. "Follow your heart" was what we wanted to do but the band went to another state for a series of shows and I had only telephone calls to look forward to.

A couple of months went by and one day Kevin showed up at our door. I was working with Father at the store when Mother called to ask if I could come home a little early and bring some ice cream that Bobbie was crying for. I didn't suspect anything because we tried to keep Bobbie from getting upset if we could. Even though we tried not to make her spoiled, we almost always did what she wanted to keep her calm. She could have become a really bad child but she didn't have that disposition. She was bright and happy, a joy to everyone who knew her and the sunshine of our lives. Anyway, I popped in the kitchen door with the ice cream and there he was at the kitchen table with Bobbie and Mother, a big smile on his face and his eyes with that twinkle that I had grown to love and dreamed about at night. He took me in his arms, right there in the kitchen, swinging me around; much to Bobbie's delight. "I just had to see you," he said as we went outside together.

My first thought was that Mary was wrong. The band didn't come first...I came first. My blouse was almost splitting as my heart beat so hard. I had found love. It was even more wonderful than I had imagined it would be.

Kevin and I talked about our future that night and all the next day. He wanted me to marry him. He had talked to a music company about a full time job and would do the band part-time. The other band members understood and would go along with what he wanted to do. They were all a little tired of traveling all the time. Of course I said yes. This was what I knew life would be like. Someone to love me like Father loved Mother and a chance to have my own home and family and "live happily ever after". My parents were not too surprised but talked at length with Kevin about our future plans. Finally they agreed to the engagement and on that same old porch swing Kevin slipped a diamond ring on my finger. Even though the diamond was just a chip, it was the most beautiful ring I had ever seen. The first diamond I ever owned.

After he left, Kevin and I made plans over the phone for our wedding. Actually I made plans and told him about it over the phone. Mary was to be a bridesmaid and came several weeks before the wedding to help us get ready. We became good friends in those weeks and even she admitted that she was wrong about the importance of the band. "You just have to find the right one", she would say, "to know what is the most important." She was going to go to school in the same town where Kevin and I would live and still sing with the band when they performed so I looked forward to having her close by and watching our friendship grow.

Mother and I went through the things that she wanted me to have for my first home. We would have an apartment at first so I had to decide what things I wanted to leave behind until I had room or need for them. The baby quilt that we had made three years earlier, before Bobbie was born, went back into the cedar chest and up in the attic. In my dreams I could see a baby already with Kevin's twinkling blue eyes. How happy could one girl possibly be, I thought so many times.

Chapter Four

The day of our wedding came and on that morning as I sat in the kitchen with Mother and Father I was more than a little frightened of the future without them by my side. The fear passed as quickly as it had come. I knew that they would always be right here in this house, just a phone call away and that my life would be so wonderful that I couldn't possibly wish for more.

Everything was beautiful as Kevin and I were married in our back yard. We had transformed it into a beautiful garden with arbors, and tents with baskets of flowers everywhere. Bobbie was my flower girl and stole the show in her pretty blue dress and halo of wildflowers. Mother had embroidered a pillow for the ring bearer to carry that said "follow your heart". She had kept it a secret and gave it to me as I was putting on the wedding dress that she had worn on her wedding day. I wept tears of joy when I saw it and knew that I was following my heart. That day I pledged to love this man forever and heard him pledge his life to me. The tears I saw in my Father's eyes were tears of joy, I said to myself. Now he has the son he never had. In the back of my mind I was thinking that maybe one day Kevin could take over the store and we could live next door and grow old on the same old street. So many dreams floated around that day and so many memories that are with me still.

Our life together began in a tiny apartment in a big city. It wasn't too far away from my hometown but seemed like another world to a small town girl. The traffic was a nightmare and the city noises made me grateful for all the quiet nights on the porch in my girlhood. We were so in love and all the other things were unimportant. Kevin continued to work in the music store and booked engagements for the band on most weekends. This left me with a lot of time to spare. I lovingly folded his clothes, smelling the scent of him on the bedclothes and secretly putting my head on his pillow and remembering how much I loved him lying there beside me. I learned all his favorite dishes and spent a lot of time cooking meals to please him. He always seemed happy when we were together and our first few months were perfect.

Mary was enrolled in the local Junior College, taking business courses and she encouraged me to go with her. I had done a little of the bookkeeping for Father in the store and had some talent with numbers. We could use the extra income so I became a student again.

The months went by fast and I was less and less homesick as time passed. Mother called often, with Bobbie always having to tell me some adventure she had at preschool or with her friends. It brought back memories and I was so glad that she was having the happy childhood with Mother and Father that I was so fortunate to have had. Father always wanted to "help us out" financially but I declined. We needed to learn to make it on our own, I thought. Kevin wanted more equipment for the band and we were always saving for a new guitar or speakers or money for road trips. He enjoyed the band so much and it gave me pleasure to see how much it meant to him.

I finished my college courses and went for interviews for a job. It was scary but exciting and a good experience for me to meet strangers and be comfortable with them. Mary helped me get the proper "work clothes", and learn how to interview. But before I actually got a job I found out that I was going to have a baby! I could hardly wait to tell Kevin. He, of course, was concerned but we had always said that we wanted a family. The band gave us a big party and everyone was excited with us. Don and Iris already had a little boy, just a few months old and we laughed and said we were starting the next generation of musicians to carry on the band. Mother and Father, and especially Bobbie were thrilled with the news and wanted me to come home to have the baby.

Kevin spent more and more time with the band, booking more gigs and building up the inventory of music and equipment. I began to spend time with Iris and her baby while the men were out on the road. Mary continued to sing with the band and worked their schedule around her new office job.

Iris confided in me her concern that the band was occupying more and more time for the men and that they were in debt because of lost hours on the regular job. Kevin was aggravated when I mentioned this to him. He felt that Iris was being a whiner and unduly upsetting me. I knew that the band was important and I remembered that Mary had told me it would always come first, but I knew our finances were OK and that Kevin was as excited about home and family as I was, so I just changed the subject when Iris wanted to talk about the band.

I just wanted to hear about the baby. It was all new to me and I spent as much time as I could helping her take care of her son and dreaming of the day when my own arrived.

We had decided that I would go home to have the baby and stay a few weeks so that Mother could help me and Kevin would not miss any work. A couple of weeks before my due date we packed the car and took the short trip back home.

It was good to be back in my own room with all the familiar things around but different too. My new life was with my husband and soon to be child. But, it was great to be the center of attention at home and to share the excitement of the event with these people I loved. Kevin went back to the city and Mother, Bobbie and I started counting the days till "Baby Day", as Bobbie called it.

One rainy afternoon as we were looking at all the tiny little clothes we had gathered, Mother brought out the quilt. I had forgotten about it and so many memories flooded my mind as we looked at all the little squares again. It seemed so long ago that we had made the quilts. Mother's baby had gotten so big.

Bobbie brought her quilt from her room and we laughed as she climbed in the crib and pretended to be a baby again. She had come a long way from the sick little newborn to a busy kindergarten student. Her heart was still weak and there were a lot of things she couldn't, and would never do. Mother watched her carefully and she was a happy child, not missing the running and rough playing that she had never done.

I put the quilt in the suitcase to take to the hospital along with a beautiful little batiste dress and tiny crocheted booties from Iris to take for our baby's first outfit.

As the days went slowly by, as they do when you are waiting for something special to happen, I began to notice how tired Mother looked and acted. She had a doctor's appointment while I was there and said it was routine and I was not to worry about it. Father had found a lady to come in once or twice a week to help out with the heavy cleaning and this surprised me. I ask him about it one night as we sat on the old familiar porch. I was in the wicker rocker since I didn't fit the swing lately. He didn't make too much of it either, just said he felt that Mother had deserved a little rest. Caring for Bobbie had been an extra burden on her. A burden of love, she called it, but still a burden. I promised that I would not let her do too much for us while we were there. It seemed like old times, Father and I sharing secrets on the porch after supper. Some of the neighbors even came by like in the old days and stopped to see how we were doing and asking when the baby was due, how my life in the city was and when Kevin was bringing me back home.

I missed my husband, so we spent too much money on the telephones, and a couple of days before the baby's arrival date he came to be with us. I flew, as easily as a small elephant could fly, into his arms and never wanted to be away from them again. He and Father spent some time together at the store the next couple of days and I began to secretly wish that we might really be coming back here to live. I knew in my heart that Kevin wasn't ready to give up his dreams for the band but it was a good feeling to wish anyway. My dream of my life as it had always been was crowded out with the reality that my life was with Kevin and the baby wherever we were. As long as the three of us were together, my life would be perfect.

The day of my baby's birth is one of those clear memories, I talked about earlier. The first signs of labor, the trip to the hospital, leaving Kevin with Mother and Father in the waiting room. All these things are as if they happened yesterday. When she was born and the doctor said she was healthy and beautiful I knew that from that moment on my life would be complete. What more could a woman want than a man who loved her and a beautiful daughter to share their love.

Kevin was thrilled with his new child too. He counted the fingers and toes and laughed at how much she looked like him, especially around the eyes. Mother, Father and Bobbie couldn't stay away from her. After we came back from the hospital they would make trip after trip to my room to watch her sleep in the crib that had been mine and then Bobbie's. Mother spent a lot of time in Granny's old rocker with her granddaughter wrapped in the quilt. Slowly rocking and looking at the beautiful little face.

Kevin brought Mary and Iris and Don, with their baby to our daughter's baptism. We all stood at the baptismal fount and repeated the baptismal promises and hearing her name for the first time as the priest said, "I baptize you, Catherine Elaine, in the name of the Father, and of the Son, and the Holy Spirit, Amen."

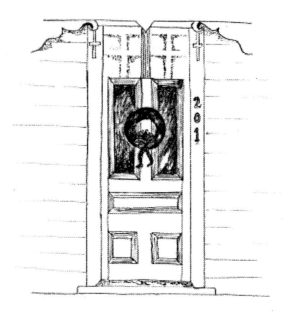

Chapter Five

All too soon it was time for me to take Catherine and join Kevin. I had depended on Mother to make all the decisions for Catherine's care and now was anxious to have her all to ourselves. Surely, our little family of three was the happiest in the world. Mother, Father and Bobbie stood on the porch and waved long after our car was out of sight. I was so excited about going on with our lives that I did not even look back at these people I loved so deeply. The parents that had given me the most important thing that any child could ask for, love unconditional. I was just following my heart as I held Catherine, wrapped in her quilt with the heart border. If I had known then what was to happen, I would have looked back as long as I could see the three standing there on the old familiar porch.

For a few short weeks we lived a fantasy life. Kevin went to work each morning, Catherine and I had time to get to know each other. I so wanted our relationship to be like the one I had with my Mother from the very beginning. Kevin seemed to enjoy her and was excited at all the things a baby this young could do but the band was growing and he was home for short periods and away to practice or perform. I was amazed at how much equipment they had acquired and how fast they were becoming the big band they wanted to be. More and more of the jobs were further away and they were making a name for themselves all over the south.

Iris and I spent more and more time together as they men were away. We took turns baby-sitting both children so there was time for each to have time alone. I didn't really want to be away from Catherine for very long, but an hour now and then to buy groceries or window shop was welcomed. The memory of these weeks are some of the cloudy memories. They went by so fast and so much happened afterwards that I can scarcely remember the first month of Catherine's life.

Kevin came home one night so excited that I hardly recognized him. He had been offered a job performing with the band in England! "England?", I said. "How could you ever do that?

It would cost a fortune to fly to a foreign country, not to mention the number of people and band instruments you would have to transport." We had never discussed our financial situation. Kevin paid all the bills from his job at the music store and had money left over to support the band. I had always been proud of the way he handled things and never felt the need to question it. He became angry when I started asking how we could do this with a young child. Mothers didn't go to work and leave children a month old with strangers. "Don't ask me to do that!" I shouted, becoming angry and a little frightened too. We spent a couple of days not talking about the offer and I thought that he had realized that it was an impossible dream.

How can your life change completely without your being able to make it stop? No matter how hard you wish and pray that things are not happening, they do happen and you are helpless to control any of it.

I received a telephone call early one morning, well before dawn! It was my father. I could hardly understand him, he was crying uncontrollably and going from almost whispering to shouting. Mother was dead! As long as I live I will hear those words and feel their pain. She had a heart condition, he said, didn't want me to worry. It had started when Bobbie was born and they had been watching and medicating and thinking it was under control. That night Father had sensed something wrong when he woke up to find she was not in the bed beside him. He found her in my old room, in Granny's rocker. He was calling her doctor and the police as they would need to investigate a sudden death. "Could I come right away?" What a question, yes I could come and would be on my way in minutes.

Kevin was with the band performing out of town. They were expected back the next day. I called Iris and frantically explained to her what had happened. She suggested that I leave Catherine with her so I could get off right away. Kevin would be back in the morning and could bring her with him. He would be coming as soon as possible we knew.

I drove the miles that night in a daze. What kind of bad dream was this? My Mother was always going to be there. She would be on the porch waiting for me and asking where her grandchild was! This thought got me through the night and only when I pulled in the driveway and saw all the police cars and people standing around the house did I realize that it was really a bad dream that somehow had come true.

The only part I didn't know as I climbed the steps to my childhood home was that the bad dream was a long way from being over. A deputy from the police department, who had been my Father's friend for years gently took me by the arm as I opened the front door and led me out to the swing. I remember that the wisteria was blooming and the swing was enclosed in a flowery canopy of purple and green. Anytime I smell the sweet fragrance of wisteria now this memory comes flooding back. As we sat down I ask where Bobbie was. "Next door at a friend's", he told me. "I have some news that you must hear before you go in," he continued. "I understand that your Father called you and told you about your Mother's heart attack. We were able to determine that it was just that and that she died peacefully. But the part that I wish I didn't have to tell you is that your Father followed her in less than two hours." What was he saying? I couldn't hear him for the noise that suddenly filled my mind. It was the pounding of my own heart as I tried to understand what he was saying, Followed her? Followed her?

Before the police had arrived Father had taken Bobbie, half asleep, to the neighbors' and come back to wait for them. He was on the porch swing when they came out and gave him their findings. The deputy said he nodded and didn't speak when they told him they would send an ambulance to take her away as soon as they could contact them. Maybe someone should have stayed with him but he didn't seem to want to talk to anyone and they left him there. The deputy said he looked back and felt so sorry for his old friend who had lost the love of his life. Why didn't I look back the last time I was here? The thought passed through my mind as the deputy continued.

"Less than an hour later the ambulance arrived to take your Mother's body to the funeral home and not getting an answer when they knocked, they went into the house and to the room where we had told them she was. There they found your Father. He sat on the floor in front of the rocking chair and apparently had a heart attack also. His head was in her lap and he was holding her hand in both of his. "Died of a broken heart", was the expression I heard over and over.

Now I was the adult, no longer the child of these two people, I had all the decisions to make and for the rest of my life I had to rely on the things that they had taught me to take care, not only of myself without their guidance, but to take care of Bobbie also. Now I knew why she had a weak heart, she had inherited it from both of them.

I called Iris as soon as I could and was reassured that Catherine was fine. She would try to contact the band and she knew Kevin would be there as soon as possible. Somehow I found the strength to take care of all the things you must do for a funeral and see that

Bobbie was OK. She was too young to know what had really happened but she knew that she would not see her mother and father again. It was she and I now and my assurance that she would always be a part of mine and Kevin's family and help us raise Catherine gave her a little something to look forward to.

I closed the store, not knowing what I would do about that or anything else. I waited for Kevin to come and knew that when he held me in his arms my strength would return and I would be able to go on.

When the day of the funeral arrived, so did he. He was very quiet and I wondered if he had formed a bond with Father that I was not aware of. He didn't bring Catherine, much to my dismay. He and Iris had decided that I had so much to handle that it would be easier to let her stay there a few more days. Kevin left that afternoon, hurrying to get back to our child and his job. I felt the emptiness of the old house even more after he left and Bobbie and I spent the night together in her room, lying close to each other in the darkness of the night and in the darkness that now was our lives.

So many things needed to be taken care of. I called each day to check on the baby and was reassured that she was fine, I wouldn't recognize her when I got home as she was growing daily, Kevin was taking her at night and Iris was doing fine during the days. As much as I wanted to take Bobbie and run away and leave all the past behind I knew that we would need to sell the store and house. I had the responsibility of taking care of Bobbie for the rest of her life and not knowing what kind of medical bills we would have or how much it cost to raise a child, I determined that I had no choice but to see it through.

The thought came to me that maybe this was the time for Kevin, Catherine and I to come back home. Yes! That was the perfect solution. Kevin could run the store, I could do the book work. Bobbie could continue with her school and doctors where she was known. Catherine could grow up in the same house, with the same love that was holding me together now. This was perfect!

I placed a call to the music store hoping too catch Kevin before he left to pick up Catherine. I thought I had dialed the wrong number when the girl answering the phone said that Kevin no longer worked there. In fact, she had taken his job when he left." Several days ago", she said. My heart raced, maybe he had thought of the same thing and was on his way to me. Everything was going to be OK now I told myself and began to get excited about seeing both of them again, my precious baby, would she know me? would she be as happy as I was in this house? When would they come? My thoughts raced ahead and I almost told Bobbie the good news. Something stopped me though and I thought maybe Kevin and I should make some decisions before we tell her.

I called Iris when I had time to calm down from the excitement of the moment. She did not answer but I didn't think anything of it. She was probably glad to have Kevin take Catherine away and had taken her son out to the park or maybe was at our apartment helping Kevin pack. Sure, that's where they are. I'll call there.

When the operator told me that the telephone at our apartment had been disconnected I was more sure than ever that they were on their way "home". Bobbie and I cooked a real meal for the first time since the funeral. Ham and sweet potatoes, green bean casserole, even an apple pie by Mother's old recipe. She didn't question why we were cooking so much and I didn't tell her what I suspected. Let it be a surprise I thought. The child needed a good thing to happen in her life for a change. She had been doing really good and was helping me to hold up seeing how much like Mother she was.

Chapter Six

We ate some of the supper that night and when midnight came I left the porch swing and tried to sleep listening to every night sound. Was that the car? Was Catherine hungry by now? Had they stopped at a rest stop and fallen asleep? All the bad things that can happen to a traveler came to mind as I lay there waiting for something? What?

The next morning I decided that I had to find them. Bobbie was to spend the night with some school friend and I made arrangements for her to stay until Sunday. Filling Father's car with gas and taking clothes for overnight I locked the front door of the old house and started out on the most incredibly unbelievable journey of my life.

The first surprise came when I reached our address. There was a "for rent" sign in the yard and no sign of any of our things around. My next stop was at Iris and Don's. There too I found a "for rent" sign and nothing to remind me that they had been here. Where was my family?

I drove to a local Waffle House to get something to eat, I had left home early and driven most of the morning. Over a cup of coffee I tried to think what to do next? I was so used to Kevin or my parents making decisions for me that I wasn't sure if I knew what the next move was.

I placed a call to the next door neighbor to my parent's house to be sure Kevin and I had not passed each other on the way. No, they had not seen anyone, They would let him in if he came and for me to call back and check whenever I wanted to.

My next stop was the real estate office. There I learned that Kevin had given them notice over a week ago that he was leaving, actually the day after my parents died. He told them that we were leaving the country. I couldn't believe what I was hearing. What was he thinking? My parents had been dead less than a day and he thought I was leaving the country? I found that Iris and Don had given notice the same day to vacate their apartment. Iris had never mentioned it to me during all the telephone calls about the baby's welfare. What was going on? This seemed so unreal. The most unreal part was that my child was gone and I had no idea where she was.

Mary was gone as well as all the other members of the band. Could they have taken my baby to England? How was this possible?

Not knowing what else to do, I drove back to Oak Hill. As the tires made their sounds on he highway my mind kept turning over and over, where is she? What has Kevin done? Why would he do this? We could have talked about it? Catherine and I could have stayed with Bobbie while he was away? Surely I will have some word from him when I get home. But there was nothing there to greet me when I drove up in the old familiar driveway.

37

I decided that I could not find them alone. I made an appointment with Father's friend in the police department and tearfully told him the whole story. You can imagine his surprise. He called the police department in the town where we had lived and filed a missing persons report for Kevin. They would not file one for Catherine for, supposedly, she was with her father. I just had to wait, he told me. Maybe I would hear from them soon. He talked of my parents and how much courage they had and he knew that I had some of that same courage too. I thanked him for his kindness but I knew that he was wrong, I didn't have that kind of courage, I was scared to death! I had no idea that he was also wrong about my hearing from them, I did not!

The days turned into weeks and no word came about Kevin and Catherine. I called Mary's parents who told me that the band was indeed going to England, probably had already gone. They didn't hear from her often but if they did hear or get an address they would call me. I didn't want to tell them the whole story, I still couldn't believe that Kevin had done this. That I knew so little about him. Why he would want to take a two month old baby along just didn't make sense.

As I waited I spent my days trying to get the store settled. It was needed in our small town and I had opened it back up as soon as I could. One of the old employees was running it for me and was interested in buying it. I knew that I had to go over the books and see what we had invested before I could even suggest a selling price. Luckily I had taken that college course right after our marriage and was familiar with the bookkeeping system.

One night as I sat at the dining room table with Father's books laid out before me I discovered that from the beginning of our marriage Father had been giving Kevin money. One after another disbursements was "To Kevin" several hundred dollars at the time, right up until the time of Father's last entry before he died.

I sat there for a long time, trying to make sense out of this. Why did Father give Kevin money? I knew that he had asked me if we needed help to get started but I refused, saying that Kevin managed our money well and that we were doing OK. Had he asked Kevin? Did Kevin ask him? All the time I was so proud that Kevin could take care of us and build up the band he was taking money from Father. Did I know this man at all? This man who had my child somewhere! The last entry was for five thousand dollars. Was that the trip to England money? Surely if Kevin had told Father that he was going to England Father would have called me to bring Catherine and come home. Did Kevin not tell Father the truth? I became more and more frightened that I may never see either of them again. I must do something, I can't just sit here the rest of my life not knowing where they were But what!

Chapter Seven

By the time I had sold the store I knew that I could not find Catherine from here. I had the leave the comfort of the porch swing and go looking. We closed the house and Bobbie and I went to Atlanta. What a momentous move this was. I had never been to a big city, especially one so far away. I had thought about what I would have to do to find my baby and I knew that I would have to do it, no matter the costs.

Bobbie and I found a small apartment in the city and I enrolled her in a good school where they were aware of her heart condition. I wanted to spend as much time as possible trying to find my family but I knew that sooner or later I would have to find a job.

For months I followed every lead I could find. I went to clubs and talked to band members that might have know Kevin's band. They had heard of them, but not lately. One thing I did find out was that if they indeed went to England, they probably left from here. This made me even more determined to keep looking but the money from the store had to last us for the rest of our lives so I started looking for a job.

I worked in several accounting firms but had difficulty keeping up with the work hours and taking care of Bobbie. Most companies did not care if you had a child at home when they wanted you to work overtime. So I moved several times from job to job.

41

As the first anniversary of our move to Atlanta came I found the perfect job. It was with Bobbie's doctor, not too much older than I. He was looking for someone to keep his books and understood my situation with Bobbie at home. As we worked together he often suggested that I bring Bobbie to the office when I had to work late or on weekends.

Time went by and I made little progress in my search. I never gave up hope that someday I would find them and reclaim my child. In the meantime I had to believe that Kevin was taking care of her and giving her the love that I could not give. I hoped that Iris was with them and taking care of her along with her son.

One Saturday as Bobbie played in the office and I caught up on some work Dr. Leonard's wife stopped by to check on some drapes she was replacing in the waiting room. He had mentioned her many times and we had met at the Christmas party for the staff but I had not had the opportunity to get to know her at all. She brought their little daughter along and I was so envious of their relationship. The child was about three. A beautiful little girl with golden curls and blue-blue eyes. I couldn't help but think about my own little Catherine who was just a little younger than her Ellen. Did she have curls? Was she this happy?

After that day Mrs. Leonard and I talked often on the telephone, about the business as well as about Bobbie's heart condition. She had a similar condition and was able to help me through some rough times when medication needed changing and questions came up at school. We became friends and when she asked me to call her Katherine instead of Mrs. Leonard, I could hardly breathe. I had decided not to tell anyone about my search for Catherine. It was such a personal thing and so disappointing as there were no leads.

The girls became friends too and we let them spend the night together at our place once in a while. I felt comfortable letting Bobbie go to the park or to a movie with them because Katherine knew what to do in an emergency. Luckily the emergencies were getting farther and farther apart and Bobbie was becoming a happy little girl once again. We talked often about Mother and Father and knew in the back of our minds that the old house was still there and we could return whenever we wanted to. Mother and Father would always be there in our hearts.

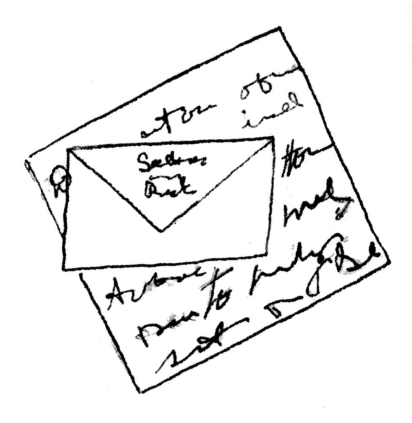

Chapter Eight

As before, my life changes came in dramatic ways, leaving me with a sense of no control. I had put Bobbie to bed one night and settled with coffee in front of the fireplace to open the mail, which I had neglected for a couple of days. One envelope had a foreign stamp but no return address. It had been forwarded from my parent's old address. As I opened it a newspaper article fell out. I picked it up off the carpet and read the headline." Band Members Die in Plane Crash". I dropped it again and had to make myself pick it up and read on, not wanting to know but not being able not to know. The article said that a local band, traveling in their private plane, had crashed on an English hillside killing all aboard, including a small child. No names were available as most of the band members were American. Someone had written, "so sorry" across the bottom. I started to cry and all the years of frustration poured from me. This nameless child was my little girl, almost three, dead on some English hillside. She had never known her Mother, she had never been given the chance to know her aunt Bobbie who would have loved her so. So many chances were gone for her now, all her chances. As my tears dried up my anger at Kevin set in. How could he have taken my child to her death when she could have had such a good life with me. We could have planted flowers, made cookies in Mother's kitchen, both of us covered with flour and laughing at each other. We could have spent many happy hours on the swing while I told her the story of the "follow your heart" quilt. Was that quilt there beside her burned body on the English hillside? Damn you Kevin! How could I have ever loved you? How could you have forgotten the pledges we made to each other on our wedding day or the promises we made at Catherine's baptism?

I sat there as the fire died to embers and sometime before morning I realized that my search was over and I had to go on with life. I could not bring Catherine back. I could not undo the things that Kevin had done to my life, but Bobbie needed me now and for her I had to put it away in my heart somewhere and go on. I'd always follow my heart I guess, even after doing that had brought me so much pain. I said a prayer that night and asked for guidance and strength to do what I needed to do for my life and my sister.

It is always hard to believe that the world keeps on turning. or as the lyrics of a popular song at the time says, "how does the sun keep on shining?". But it did and the seasons changed and the months turned into years. My work and my life caring for Bobbie kept me going. I did not have anyone to confide in about the things that had happened to my family. I waited to hear from the English government about the plane crash but no word came. I almost talked to Dr. Leonard about what to do but thought better of it. After all he was just my employer. The relationship with Katherine and Ellen was comforting to me, but I didn't know her well enough to tell her about Kevin and my Catherine. Because of the girls we began to see each other more often. Ellen would spend weekends with us when Katherine and Dr. Leonard, Bill as I was told to call him in private, wanted some time away. They went to Texas often, to see family I assumed. Once in a while I would let Bobbie visit them. Their home was a beautiful, warm place and filled with so much love that she adored being there and with their family. My heart ached for the loss she must have felt for Mother and Father and the love that she had always been surrounded with when they were alive. It was easy to love her. Bobbie was such a friendly child, wise beyond her years and always making anyone around he feel that they were special. Katherine mentioned this to me on several occasions after they had spent some time with her. She seldom mentioned their similar heart condition, but occasionally when I mentioned the medication changes and Bobbie's progress, she would admit that her own condition was always changing. Some medications worked, some didn't.

My relationship at the office was one to be envied, Dr. Leonard gave me full reign to keep his records and the hours I spent in the quiet, well run practice were calming to my soul. I was shocked sometimes to realize that hours had gone by without my thinking or mourning the losses I have suffered.

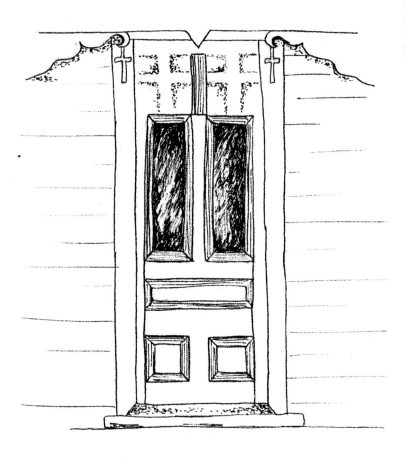

Chapter Nine

When vacation time came Bobbie and I decided to go back home and check on the old house and some other business with the store and bank. When we mentioned it to Katherine Ellen begged to come with us. I wasn't sure that I could handle a child her age in the car but Katherine offered to pay our plane fare down and said it would be a big help to her if we would take Ellen with us. She and Bill had a trip to Texas that week and didn't like leaving Ellen with anyone else.

We rented a car and drove to our little town. It was a bitter sweet homecoming. The place was so empty without our parents. Bobbie and Ellen ran for miles around the big back yard and explored every nook and cranny of the old house. They even begged to go into the attic but I put them off until I had time to go up with them. Everything was in good shape with the property. An uncle who lived next door took care of it for us. He suggested that we might like to sell it or at least rent it while we were away but I couldn't imagine anyone else in Mother's kitchen or in their bedroom. In the back of my mind I always intended to come back someday to live and let Bobbie go to the same schools I did and hopefully have the same kind of teen years that I was so fortunate to have.

I talked to Father's friend, Sheriff Davis, one night about the situation with Kevin. I showed him the newspaper clipping and he promised to investigate and see what he could find out for me. He wasn't sure that he could do anything, but it was a relief just to tell someone.

Of course memories were everywhere. Everywhere I looked there were memories of my childhood, the teen years and even the brief time Kevin and I spent there. The nursery where Bobbie and then Catherine spent their first days still held the crib and rocker that we had so lovingly placed there. The blue walls reminded me of the "little brother" that I had been promised. How could I have loved any child more than I loved and needed Bobbie. Catherine only spent a short time in this room but I could smell the powder, the sweet smell of her hair as I rocked her to sleep and I could hear the music of the night outside the window as the crisp white curtains blew in the late afternoon breezes. I could remember the thoughts I had as I watched my child during those early days. The plans I made for Kevin, Catherine and I. The voice of Mary crept into my thoughts saying, "The band always will come first". I couldn't indulge in self-pity for very long. Two little girls called up to me from the bottom of the stairs, "when can we eat?".

Katherine called to see if we had made the trip safely and was surprised that Ellen didn't even want to talk to her on the telephone. I made her listen to her Mother's voice for a minute and heard Katherine say, "Mommie and Daddy love you precious and will forever. You are my life precious baby, have a good time but remember Mommie is waiting for a hug." That night as we sat on the porch, all three of us in the swing, Ellen wrapped her chubby baby arms around me and said, "Ellen loves you. Bobbie too." This was the beginning of many times we shared the swing but this is the one that I remember the most.

Chapter Ten

The day we were to fly back home, after our week was over, we received a telegram from Houston, Texas. Telegrams always scare people and I was nervous since I didn't know anyone in Texas. "Please keep Ellen at your place until you hear from me. Katherine not able to return, Will call your apartment Wednesday." Signed Bill.

We flew back to the apartment. I didn't tell the girls anything about the message, just that Ellen could stay with us a little while more. The girls were excited to be able to play longer, they chatted all the way back about what they would do and how much they had missed Bobbie's dolls and toys.

Bill called Wednesday. Katherine had gone to Houston, as she often did to see a heart specialist but had had a heart attack while being examined. She was in the Cardiac Care Unit and he could only see her for a few minutes at the time. Being a heart specialist himself made him more anxious because he knew the complications that could arise. He assured me that he was fine, relieved that Ellen was being cared for and would let us know when they would be returning. I was to call the receptionist at the office and have her cancel his appointments for the rest of the week. My mind raced as I got the children feed, bathed and off to bed. They could feel that I was nervous about something but I told them it was just the airplane flight and getting settled back into our lifestyle, but I would stay at home with them for a few days and we would do some fun things together. This sent them off to bed with smiles.

I sat in the darkness after they were asleep thinking about Bill and Katherine. They were so much in love. Not that they made a big display of it, but the times I was with them it was so obvious. Like Mother and Father, and like I had dreamed Kevin and I would be.

The phrase, till death do us part", turned round and round in my head as I tried to sleep that night. Was I frightened for Bill and Katherine or remembering my own love? Sometime before morning the telephone woke me. I could hardly recognize Bill's voice. Memories of my Father's last conversation with me almost made me scream into the telephone. Katherine had died. Her heart weakened by years of struggle, finally gave out. She was only thirty-five, how could this happen? He was in so much pain and there was nothing I could do for him. I assured him that Ellen would be all right with Bobbie and me for as long as necessary and promised to make some other calls for him around town. There was another doctor who would take care of his practice for a while. When I hung up the telephone I could hardly breathe. How could this happen to two people who were so much in love? Why did I doubt that? Wasn't my mother and father in love? Didn't I love Kevin. There are no answers to these kinds of questions but the pain of them remains with us always.

When Katherine's body was returned to the city I took Ellen home and got her clothes and toys and helped Bill prepare her for the loss of her Mother. I think Bobbie helped more than we did because she was able to make Ellen understand that things would be OK. She had been through the same loss and Ellen clung to her for days when no one else could reach her.

I kept her with Bobbie and I for a month. I worried about Dr. Leonard being in his house alone but he insisted that he needed to be there. He plunged into his practice with more fervor than usual. It was as if he alone had to find a cure for heart disease. It broke my heart to see him at the office and on the nights that he visited with Ellen he could only hold her with tears running down his face. We both knew that this was a temporary situation but it seemed the right one for us all.

As time for Bobbie to return to school drew near I had to broach the subject to him. What would Ellen do by herself? The sitter I hired for them during the summer would be returning to college. There were decisions to be made. Ellen protested violently when we suggested that she had to go back to her own house soon. I told Bill this one night when he came to take us to dinner and spend some time with his daughter. We had just put the girls to bed and over coffee were talking about what we should do. Bill stayed most of the night that night. He began talking about their life together. I was uncomfortable at first because I wasn't family, or even close friend, but then I realized that he

55

needed to talk about it, just as I had so needed someone to talk about Kevin to.

Their life had been almost storybook material. College sweethearts, they had gone through their careers together. Katherine finished nursing school first and they had married while he was still in medical school. Getting settled into his practice and paying off all the school expense had taken up most of their time the first few years of their marriage. I was glad that we were sitting in semi-darkness as I was aware of the pain it was causing to remember these times. He admitted, as most people will, that the "hard times" looking back were the "good times." He talked about building their dream house and knew that he could never sell it. Even if he and Ellen didn't need that much space, it was to forever be her home. He finally came to the part in their story about Katherine's health. She had discovered in school that she had a heart disease. He even made that his specialty because he knew that one day he would heal her. He had devoted many hours to research and consulted hundreds of doctors but "in the end he might as well have spent the time at home with her." he said. I reminded him of Bobbie, and all the other patients of his who were still benefiting from his study and reassured him that Katherine was proud of the work he was doing and would not have wanted him to spend time with her when he could be making progress in his research.

"That is why she liked you so much", he said, "She told me so many times that you could look right into a person's heart and see and say the right thing You brought her a lot of comfort, you know." This took me by surprise. I knew that Katherine and I got along famously, but I would never have thought of her talking to Bill about me. Changing the subject because of my embarrassment, I asked about Ellen's role in their life. "Were you afraid when Katherine had a child? Do you fear that she inherited her Mother's weak heart?" There were a lot of questions I wanted to ask because Katherine and I had never talked about Ellen's birth. I don't think I would have shared "labor stories" or anything with her because she did not know that I also had a child. That story was too painful and humiliating to tell.

As Bill began to talk about Ellen and Katherine he smiled for the first time. Katherine had wanted a baby for a long time. All the medical evidence said that this was too risky and he had tried every medical argument he knew to dissuade her to no avail. Finally he said, he had resorted to the argument that he didn't need a child to complete their love. He could not risk losing her for anything. With an even wider smile he continued, "But then it happened and I realized that I was wrong. She needed this child, I guess I did too. Ellen brought out the very best in both of us and completed the circle of love that we had begun. I realize that I would have risked everything I hold dear for this to happen. Katherine's last three years were the happiest anyone could have. As for Ellen's heart, there is a slight chance that she may have the condition, but I monitor it closely and will as long as I live. She is what I have left of Katherine.

I wanted at that moment to tell him that I knew the love he felt, that I also had known the love of a child. That the month that I had been allowed to spend with her was one of the most precious of my memories but the one that cut me to the heart at each remembrance of it. But, I could not tell him or anyone. It was something that I had to hold in my own heart. Even Bobbie had stopped asking and talking about Catherine. So many other things now filled her life that the memory was gone. But not for me. My baby, taken from me so soon, will haunt me as long as I live.

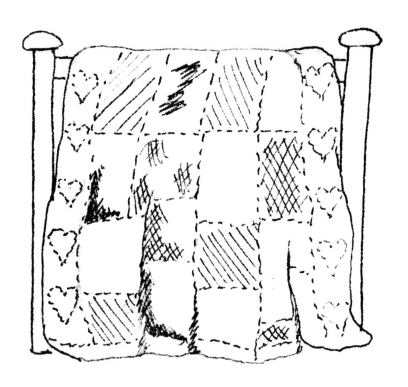

Chapter Eleven

What to do about Ellen was on our minds and a few days later Bill asked me to bring Ellen and Bobbie to the house for supper. His housekeeper, a dear lady who had been with them since before Ellen's birth, would cook for us and we had some decisions to make.

The girls were excited to be back at the house and immediately, after a delicious meal, went up to play with the long neglected toys in the playroom. Bill, Mrs. Smith and I sat at the table with our coffee. I had always enjoyed being at the house. It was a beautiful three story federal-style brick. It was in one of the nicest of Atlanta's old neighborhoods. Far enough away from the busy traffic but close enough for Bill to get to his office and the hospital easily. I was admiring the beautiful furnishings and the lovely table settings when I realized that Bill was talking. Embarrassed, I looked up and realized that he was talking to me.

"I have thought about my situation with Ellen for some time now and have a proposition to present to you. I hope that you will consider it as I think that it is what is best for Ellen, and for you and Bobbie as well." What could involve Bobbie and I in his plans for Ellen?" I thought. He continued, "Would you consider moving here with Mrs. Smith and I. There are several rooms on the third floor that we have never used. They would make a nice space for you two. You would each have your own room, baths, plenty of closets and a small sitting room with a fireplace for the times you want to be alone. My plan is that Mrs. Smith will continue on with the cleaning and cooking and take care of the girls when you and I are at work. Of course, you know that I spend a lot of time after and before office hours at the hospital or in the research lab, so you will be with the girls much more than I. I have talked this over with Mrs. Smith and she thinks it is a great solution to our problem. Before you decide, remember how much Ellen loves you already and how much she will learn from having you and Bobbie here. I know that Katherine would be pleased that the examples you would set for Ellen would be the same as the ones that she would have set if she were here. We had a little saying the last few years we were together that helped us make a lot of decisions, 'follow your heart'. Don't know where it came from but it had a good track record of success for us."

It took me a while to take this all in, but the last sentence Bill said made the decision easy for me to consider. I told him that I would think about it over the week end and that if we decided to make this move we would have a lot to work out. What would the office employees think about the accountant living in the doctor's house. He knew that not much missed them, and they would have a heyday with this. "Take all the time you want", he said. "Don't let the gossip make any difference. We know what the situation will be and what is best for the girls is really the important thing."

I got little sleep that night. The memory of Mother and I talking about following your heart kept going around and around in my head. Was this the right thing for Bobbie? Would I learn to love Ellen too much so that when Bill found another love I would be torn away from her? He was a young attractive man and there were scores of women who would be setting their sites for this eligible widower.

The next morning I called Mrs. Smith and asked her to please be candid with her thoughts. I knew her well enough to know that she would tell me what she really thought. She had had a few more days than I to think about it and was wholeheartedly in favor of it. My concern about Ellen made her chuckle. "My dear," she said, it is easy to see that you already love her. How can you not be the one to help her grow into the young woman her mother would have wanted her to be."

So my life changed again. Bobbie and I made plans to move to the beautiful house in Ansley Park. Bill seemed so pleased and relieved that we were going to be taking care of Ellen. He left all the arrangements to Mrs. Smith and I. Seeing that the girls were registered in the proper schools; Bobbie in elementary and Ellen in preschool for three days a week was the first order of business. We bought furniture for the rooms that were to be ours. Ellen and Bobbie begged that we buy twin beds for Bobbie's room. They wanted to be together and even though Ellen had a beautiful room downstairs near her Dad, she would spend most of her time in Bobbie's room.

Soon after we moved in, Mrs. Smith and I took the girls to the north Georgia mountains for a little holiday. We had a wonderful weekend walking on the mountain trails, admiring the waterfalls and the flowers that bloomed everywhere. We made plans to plant some in the yard so that we could all enjoy seeing things grow and spend time tending something living. Thoughts of my childhood with my mother and our little flower beds rushed through my mind. At one nursery I bought a wisteria bush. The girls immediately remembered the one on the porch back home and made me promise to take them back soon. They both remembered what a good time they had on our last trip.

We didn't miss a single shop in the mountain town. The beautiful needlework of the mountain women was breathtaking. In one shop we decided to buy quilts for the twin beds. We had painted the room a beautiful shade of yellow and found "Sunbonnet Girl" quilts with colors that would be perfect on the white beds. A hand hooked rug with the same bright colors was a must.

As we drove home on Sunday afternoon we were looking forward to seeing our purchases in their proper places and pleased with our choices. During our conversation Mrs. Smith said, "Could you believe the handwork in those quilts? It must have taken a long time to do that. Have you ever made a quilt?" My eyes began to blur as I thought about the summer that mother and I pieced and quilted the twin baby quilts. How could we have know what life had in store for us? How lucky that we didn't know. How lucky we were to have shared that time together. I told Mrs. Smith about the quilt that we made for Bobbie and promised to show it to her sometimes. It was packed away in a trunk with Bobbie's outgrown clothes and other memories from her early years. I wished that I could tell her about the other one but the thought of it on some English hillside and the pain that memory brought me kept me from sharing it. Looking back, I realize that to have shared it with someone might have made the pain a little easier to bear.

It was a good arrangement for us all. Bobbie and Ellen grew closer to each other, like sisters. I envied their ability to share everything. Not that we were not close. We spent as much time as possible together and they shared everything with me. Bill took some time away from his work occasionally and we went to movies, the zoo and the park together. I had always felt quite comfortable with him and living in his house was not a problem to any of us. If there was talk in the office or elsewhere I never heard it.

When he was at home we often sat in the big living room downstairs or upstairs in mine after supper and after the girls were asleep. I had furnished it with beautiful oak pieces and comfortable sofa and chairs. A beautiful oak bookcase held some of the books and personal things that I had brought from home. I had brought a small piano from downstairs and the girls practiced and performed for us on occasion. Ellen was quite talented musically and Bobbie, not to be outdone, was faithful with her practice. Later she would discover the flute was more to her liking and talents and the two of them would play together quite often. With the fire ablaze in the fireplace, to warm the cool Georgia air, we spent many nights. Sometimes we talked about things the girls were doing, made some decisions that we needed to make together and some nights we didn't talk at all. We were quite comfortable just being at home.

I knew that Bill had expanded his research considerably since Katherine's death and was determined to find some answers about heart disease. He checked Bobbie and Ellen often and luckily they both were quite healthy." Happiness has a lot to do with health," he would say. They indeed were two happy little girls. Often we talked about Katherine and their life together. Once he surprised me by asking why I had never married. I told him that I was so young when my parents died and I had so much responsibility with Bobbie. Just short of the truth. "Sounds like you already know about follow your heart", he replied. Each time he used this expression my old heart ache came back. What good did that do me? But could I complain? Our life, mine and Bobbie's was a good life and she was growing up in a beautiful home with people who loved her. I didn't have the love of a husband, like my mother had, but I was happy.

Chapter Twelve

When the first Summer vacation came after our move Mrs. Smith and I took the girls back to our old home. As always the relatives had everything ready for us and we spent several weeks enjoying the small town life, the old house held so many memories for me and I found that I could share some of them with Mrs. Smith. I realized that she was probably the kind of mother to her family that mine had been to me. Her children all lived in California and were in touch often. How I longed to be able to telephone my mother and father. Images of what I would be telling them about Catherine's childhood filled my dreams as I sat in the same old swing and smelled the wisteria that summer.

Bobbie had a few flash backs of memory. She would see or smell something and come running to tell me that she remembered Mother's perfume, or planting daffodils with Father. She showed the nursery, with it's white crib and rocking chair to Mrs. Smith and proudly pointed out that it had been her room when she was "the baby". I held my breath, afraid that she would remember and mention the other baby who shared this room for only a few days. But she never said a word and my pain was mine alone.

Bill called several times while we were there and the girls begged him to come down to Oak Hill. He had several seriously ill patients and it was out of the question but he promised that next time he would come too. Ellen began noticing things that she would show him when he came.

Vacation time was over too soon and the school year started again. Ellen was in first grade and Bobbie in sixth so they were in the same school. As I dropped them off the first day I was as proud as any real mother could be of the two happy little girls, in their plaid dresses, walking hand-in-hand into a new adventure. I said a prayer of thanks for the opportunity I had been given to be a part of their lives.

My uncle died that Fall and I had to make the trip back alone to the funeral and to make arrangements for someone to look after my property. I missed the family back in Georgia but took the time away to visit old friends and family.

Father's friend in the police department ask about the search for Catherine. He had long ago given up on finding any clues to her disappearance, but thought I might have heard from some of the band members' families. He held me in a warm friendly hug as I told him that the newspaper clipping was the only clue that I had ever had. Inquiries to the English governrnent were fruitless. No bodies were ever recovered so there was no reason for them not to close the case. He reminded me again of the statement he had made the night my parents had died. "I had their strength." I wanted to believe that and looking back at how happy Bobbie was, I made myself believe that I had made some right choices for our lives.

I was making good money at my job and had been able to save quite a bit since I lived with Bill and Ellen. I decided on that trip that one day I would bring Bobbie back to go to high school where Mother, Father and I had gone. The small town life might give her the same feeling of belonging that I had to this place. We would miss Ellen but I always made myself remember that she was Bill's and not mine. I fought hard not to forget that she could be taken away any day.. hadn't Catherine.

It still amazes me that the years fly by so quickly. One morning I see a young face in my mirror, eyes ablaze with so much hope and enthusiasm for the future and then in a blink I see a grown woman, not the same eyes, nor the same enthusiasm. I had so much to be thankful for but so much to wonder about. There was no doubt in my mind that I could take care of Bobbie. She was a bright little girl and I knew that scholarships would be available when she was ready for college. But where would I be when she was grown and on her own? My feelings for Ellen were that of a Mother but my heart knew that she too would not always be a part of my life.

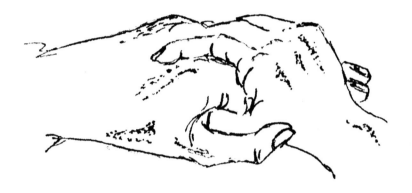

Chapter Thirteen

One night as Bill and I sat with our coffee after supper he asked if I was bothered about something. I guess my feelings had begun to show as I tried to figure out what the future held for me. As I mentioned before, I felt quite comfortable talking to him so told him what I had been thinking. "Guess it is the 30 something feelings" I said. He put his coffee cup on the table and moved to the sofa beside me before he spoke. "I am having the same feelings" he said. What will we do when the girls are grown?" I thought this was a good time to tell him that I was thinking of taking Bobbie back to our hometown in a couple of years to finish high school there. He had a shocked and worried look on his face as I spoke. He stood and walked around the beautifully appointed living room then turned and said words that I would never have dreamed he would say. "You can't mean that" How could you even think of leaving us after these years together?" He looked directly in my eyes and said, "We belong together, you know that."

I was too startled to speak for a minute. "Bill, you have never given me any impression that our relationship was anything personal. The only times we have been out have been with the girls. You have never even held my hand. Why would I think that we belonged together?"

I ran quickly up the stairs. My mind was racing. I needed to be alone. Most of the night I could not stop thinking about how he looked as he spoke to me. Did he love me? Did I love him? My mind raced back to Kevin. How much I thought I loved him and how tragic that had become. I spoke aloud to a Mother who had been gone for years, "Follow my heart, you said. How can I ever do that again?" Finally before morning I calmed down and tried to think about mine and Bill's relationship. We had so easily become a family here in his house. We enjoyed all the same things. We worked together well at the office. I really loved our quiet times together, but where was the magical feeling that I felt when Kevin kissed me? Had that died as well?

I avoided Bill at work for a couple of days and he had emergencies to keep him away until after the girls and I were in bed. The third day there was a note on my desk from Bill. He asked that I meet him after his hospital rounds for dinner. Mrs. Smith had agreed to take care of the girls for us. "We really need to talk". he wrote.

We went to a quiet little restaurant outside Atlanta. Both of us were quiet as he drove. Neither of us had a clue to what the other was thinking. After giving our order Bill reached across the table and took my hand. "This is a start", he said. "Have we never held hands before?" I smiled at his seriousness and my heart stopped beating so fast. We both seemed to relax and be our same old selves, comfortable with each other.

"You know how much I loved Katherine, don't you? I had planned to spend the rest of my life giving her anything she wanted but that's not the way it turned out. A heart disease that I could not control made other plans for my life.

What I'm trying to say, in my own clumsy way is that my life with Katherine ended a long time ago. It wasn't too long after you and Bobbie moved in that I began to realize that my new life would be with you. I guess it was so easy to enjoy each day as it came. You made things so perfect that I lazily thought this was the way it was to be. But in the past few months I have realized that what I felt was love. Not the kind of wild teen age love that I felt with Katherine, but a deep love that made me see what a wonderful woman you are and how much I want to be more than the other person in the house to you. More than your boss, more than Ellen's father. I want to be your husband, your lover, your best friend."

I could not have dreamed this conversation between us in a million years but as I looked at him and listened to his voice I realized that I too wanted more than we had. I wanted to belong to him forever. Bobbie, Ellen, none of the other things that just a little while ago were the most important things in my life mattered at that moment. I loved him too! Our dinner was barely eaten as we talked from our hearts about the years past and the life we wanted with each other.

When we returned to the house Bill took me in his arms and kissed me for the first time. Everything that had ever happened to me in the past slid from my memory as I melted in his arms with the delicious feeling of being loved. We decided to wait until the next day to try to make any plans. The feeling was too good to spoil with practical things.

Alone in my room that night thoughts of my past flooded my mind. All the things that I had kept secret. As I tried to think them through I made a decision that the would stay in my mind only. How could I ever explain to Bill about my baby. What would he think.

The next morning we lingered over breakfast after the girls had gone on a bike ride and talked about marriage and our plans for the future. I told Bill that I had been married a long time ago, right after high school but that my husband was dead. I wanted that to be in the past and wouldn't talk about it anymore. He agreed that some things were best kept unsaid. Which made me wonder what he was keeping, but I respected his privacy as he did mine.

Nancy Holland

Chapter Fourteen

The girls and Mrs. Smith were overjoyed at our news that afternoon. Mrs. Smith said that she had seen it coming for a long time and wondered why it took us so long to figure it out...

A quiet wedding was planned for December and we would all go back to the Oak Hill for the Christmas holidays. Bill had heard so much about it from our summer visits that he felt as if was his old home too.

December 5th was our wedding day. Bill and I had decided that we wanted to keep the event small and quiet. Just the family and his medical partner and wife were to witness the vows.

My mind wandered back to my first wedding day as I watched Bobbie try on her green velvet dress. She had been only three and stole the show in her blue dotted swiss dress and beautiful crown of wild flowers that mother had fashioned from the garden. She had no memory of those days and I kept my thoughts to myself. I had come to the point that I could look back at the good things that that time in my life had held and accept the bad things. Maybe my happiness at the prospect of being Bill's wife and helping him raise "our" two girls put things in a more positive perspective.

Mrs. Smith was my attendant and Bobbie and Ellen were bridesmaids in their identical green velvet dresses. As we walked down the aisle of the chapel at Saint Matthew's I knew that Mother and Father were there with us as well as Katherine. I had made a private vow that Ellen would never forget her Mother, even though she had only three years of memories I would always say and do things to remind her of Katherine's love for her. I had always done this with Bobbie. It would have been easy to take over the place of mother to both of these precious girls but I could not rob them of the memory of the mothers who loved them.

I was so proud of Bill as we stood together and heard the traditional wedding ceremony from the Book of Common Prayer. The words took on a new beauty to me as I became a wife once more. When the Rector said the final peace, "The peace of the Lord be always with you", I knew that this was the reason for my newly found joy. I knew that as Bill's wife I had found the "peace" that I had searched for so many years. The best part was that I felt that he was feeling the same. This was the way our marriage began and would continue for a lifetime.

After a small reception at our house for the office staff and a few close neighbors and friends we sat together in "our" room and talked about our wedding day. Our past was so much a part of our future that we felt quite comfortable talking about Katherine. Bill expressed his belief that she would be pleased that I was the one to care for him and for Ellen. We shared a bed for the first time that wedding night and when I awoke the next morning there beside him I knew that this was where I truly had belonged and I said a silent prayer that I would wake up every day for the rest of my life beside this good man.

Mrs. Smith went off to visit her children in California and Bill, the girls and I were off to Florida. The hometown that I loved so much took on a new face as I gave Bill the tour. "Down memory lane", I told him as we walked the familiar streets of Oak Hill and he heard the story of my early life. "What a wonderful family to grow up in", he remarked. "No wonder you turned out to be such a remarkable woman." This was indeed high praise and I beamed with pride as he squeezed my hand.

Father's grocery store had been closed for several years. New super markets had taken the place of small family businesses in all the small towns. The building now housed an Antique Store and we found ourselves looking at all the merchandise and wondering who they had originally belonged to. Each piece of furniture or jewelry that we saw had a story to tell. Secrets that would never be told unless there was a family member left in Oak Hill who knew the stories. I found a beautiful pocket watch and managed to purchase it for Bill while he was looking at some antique tools. I would sneak away and have it engraved with our wedding date before Christmas Day.

Ellen and Bill offered to go out for a tree a few days before Christmas so Bobbie and I went up into the attic to look for the decorations. It had been twelve years since she had lived here and a three year old didn't know much except that she was loved and taken care of. The visit to the attic was a bitter sweet time for me and a time of remembering for her. We found the box of ornaments and promised ourselves that we would find time to come back and go through the seemingly endless stacks of boxes that several generations had deposited there. My hope chest sat in one corner, covered now with dust, but holding so many memories that I wasn't sure I wanted to remember.

Mrs. Smith had packed some of the ornaments that Ellen and Bobbie had collected through our years together and with those we had found in the attic we discovered that we had the most beautiful Christmas tree any of us had seen. I expect that any old tree would have been beautiful to us that Christmas. Our lives were as perfect as they would ever be.

We made gingerbread and hot cider and sat in a circle on the floor around the tree. The first nineteen years of my life were spent in this room and as I looked at the people I loved the most sitting there on the old faded carpet beside me I fought back tears. I so wanted to believe that Mother and Father could somehow see us and know the happiness I felt. I thought that they would be happy that Bobbie was growing into such a wonderful, thoughtful, caring young woman. At 15 she was quite beautiful and I often saw glimpses of both our parents in her mannerisms and looks. I said a prayer of thanksgiving for the blessings I had been given and a prayer of guidance for the future that lay ahead for us all.

The girls made friends easily and by Christmas Eve they were invited to go caroling with a group of young people from the church. Bill and I took the time alone to wrap the gifts that we had bought before leaving Atlanta. I had already placed the watch under the tree. As I showed him the things I had bought for the girls he surprised me with some he had picked up also.

One gift from both of us that I knew the girls would like was identical gold crosses with their names and birth dates engraved on the back. He seemed surprised that I had the engraving done. "How did you know Ellen's birthday", he asked in surprise. "Katherine was a good organizer", I replied. She had all the birth certificates and other important papers in the safe deposit box, I guess, but there were copies in her desk also. I have used the birth certificate several times for school registrations and other things. Is there a problem with that?" "Of course not", he said, turning slightly red faced. "Guess there are a lot of things you have had to do that I didn't know about." He handed me the crosses and their delicate chains and reached over to give me a warm embrace. "I couldn't have made it through those years without you. I'll try to make the rest of our years a little easier for you."

Nancy Holland

The girls bounced into the room laughing and anxious to tell us about the new friends and how much fun caroling was. The conversation lasted until it was time for us to attend mid night services at church. It was a wonderful time and the start of a beautiful Christmas day for us all.

After New Years' day, as we closed up the house and made our plans to return to Atlanta we all agreed that we would be spending as much time as possible back in Oak Hill in the future. The girls were ten and fifteen and there was so much going on in their lives. A break back to a simpler lifestyle would be good for us all. Bill especially was enamored by the town and the people we had met. He made a trip to the hospital on the day after Christmas as was still talking about the medical people he had met and what good work they seemed to be doing there, even without all the more modern equipment that the Atlanta hospitals had.

Chapter Fifteen

It didn't take long for us to get back into our routine once the new year started. Mrs. Smith seemed glad to be back with us. I suspect we had become more family than her children by this time. She had been with Dr. Leonard and his family for seven years.

She and I spent some time redoing the living arrangements. She decided to move her rooms upstairs with the girls, leaving Bill and I with the rooms on the second floor. There was a beautiful bedroom, dressing room and a bath room bigger than the whole upstairs of Mother and Father's house in Oak Hill.

Bill was pleased with the changes we had made and worked hard at finding time to be with us as often as his busy schedule allowed. We attended the music recitals for both girls and all the school functions they were involved in. There were several week end trips alone for he and I and I looked forward to being alone with him whenever I could. The secrets of the past were always in my memory but I was slowly getting to the point that I could go for months without thinking about them. I felt quite guilty at not sharing them with Bill but couldn't find the courage to do that.

One afternoon he called to tell me that he was taking a trip to England for a conference and wanted me to go along. My heart stopped for a second. I knew that I couldn't do that. There was no way I could fly over the meadows and hillsides of England. I had nightmares of my baby lying on those meadows, with her little quilt, or what was left of it, blowing across the heather so many years ago. Luckily Bobbie was scheduled to take her SAT test the same week and I used that as an excuse for not going. She would be graduating the next year and these test would play a big part in her getting scholarships. As was his way, Bill said he understood but would miss us while he was away. I was nervous as I saw him off at the airport and relieved when he returned a few days later. He was impressed with the English countryside and wanted me to promise that we would go someday.

There were several trips back to Oak Hill in the following months. Bill was called in for consultations on several cases at the hospital there and even did surgery on two occasions. The girls and I loved each opportunity we had to go back and found it easy to renew friendships each time we were there. In the Spring as we sat in the porch swing, with the fragrance of the wisteria heavy in the early night air I felt that I had come full circle from the little girl who sat between her parents, bathed in the warmth of their love, to the woman who sat with a loving husband and that feeling of belonging all around this almost magical place.

It became harder and harder to remind the girls of their mothers. There had been so much in our lives since they had died but I continued to try to tell them of things I thought their mothers would have enjoyed or ways that they reminded me of these two wonderful women. I hoped they knew how privileged I was to be seeing the daughters they loved so much grow up into women they would be proud of.

As Bobbie's high school graduation grew near she and I began to look at colleges for her. She was a bright girl and could attend almost anywhere she wanted to. Georgia Tech was one that she had considered and as we toured the campus and talked to administration we thought back just a few years when girls could not have had this opportunity to attend. We talked about the first women who had made it possible for her and other brillant young women to become engineers and architects and chemist with diplomas from one of the best schools in the world.

There were a couple of small school over in Alabama that she was interested in also. Bill and Ellen accompanied us on several of these trips and we were reminded of how soon it would be Ellen's turn to "fly".

Chapter Sixteen

During this time Bill made more and more trips to Oak Hill. He seemed to be drawn to the smaller hospital and was making quite a name for himself with his diagnosis and treatment of some severe heart patients there. He had brought one of the younger doctors to Atlanta to spend some time with him in his research lab and office. He became almost part of our household, spending several nights a week at our dining table and with Bill in the den talking about the research and heart specialty that he was pursuing.

As we lay in our bed one night talking about our lives and the future Bill suggested that he may be interested in moving his practice to Oak Hill. He was just giving it some thought he said and wanted me to think about it as well. There was so much more time he could spend doing research and the atmosphere in the hospital was a lot like the hospital in Atlanta when he was just starting out. There was a certain calmness there that he felt comfortable with. This came as a surprise to me knowing how big his practice had become and how much he would have to arrange to make such a move.

I thought about it a lot in the next several weeks and when he wanted to talk about the possibility I sensed an excitement in his voice that I had not heard before. The years were swiftly passing by, as they do when you grow older and it was an opportunity to make some changes in our lifestyle.

We took the girls out to dinner one night and told them what we were thinking. They knew that we wanted to know what their thoughts were. This would involve us all. Much to our surprise, they were instantly excited about the possibility of living permanently in Oak Hill. They had made some good friends there on our visits and loved the smaller school scene. No decision was made but we all started thinking more seriously about it.

Of course there were a thousand things that we would have to do before we could make such a move, but when Bill was approached by a team of doctors about buying out his practice he felt that the time was right to move. His research lab could easily be moved south and the young doctor he had been training was anxious to go back home and would be a fine associate. We looked forward to Bill having more time away from a practice in his later years. There were so many things and places I wanted to introduce him to around Oak Hill. We would have to live to be one hundred to do it all.

We had no idea how we could do without Mrs. Smith but, much to our delight, she agreed to go with us. She was more like a grandmother than housekeeper. There was a small house next door to our old place that we could buy and make into a beautiful little home for her. She had not had her own place for many years and looked forward with us to the changes that our lives were about to experience.

We made arrangements to sell the big house in Atlanta but put off starting to clean it out and decide what to take and what to leave until after Bobbie's graduation.

How proud we all were of her as we sat in the auditorium and watched her receive her diploma along with her class. She was so lovely. I felt so much pride that day as I remembered the day that Mother and Father had died and I realized that they had left me the responsibility of raising this child. Luckily her heart had improved as she matured and there had not been any problems for years. Despite my inexperience in parenting, she had become more than I would have ever dreamed that day so long ago.

Ellen, at 13, was already dreaming of the day that she would be the graduate. Bill was snapping pictures of us all, as other proud families were doing, when the father of one of the other graduating seniors said to me, "That is a beautiful family you have, you must be proud of two such beautiful daughters." I smiled and replied, "Yes, they are beautiful indeed." It was difficult at times not to think of them as my daughters. I suspected that they felt the same way too. Ellen, in fact, had introduced us to her teachers as her "mom and dad" on several occasions.

Chapter Seventeen

Both girls had a job as camp counselors that summer so Mrs. Smith and I took on the task of moving while they were away. We had been in this house over ten years and Bill and Katherine five before that. It was to be an enormous job. Bill spent most of his time getting his practice in order and moving the laboratory, so Mrs. Smith and I knew that it was up to us.

Room by room we made decisions on what furniture to move. We would use some of the things that were already in the house in Oak Hill. Some pieces were so much a part of the house that there was no question about replacing them. There was Mrs. Smith's little house to furnish as well as the big attic so we kept quite a lot of things to have the movers take for us. It was quite an adventure for us all.

Often at night we would fix a light supper and sit down to share our day with Bill. There were so many decisions to make and I didn't know how attached he was to so many things. As we discussed pictures, household objects and things from Ellen's babyhood he shared his memories with us. There were moments of joy and moments of sadness as he remembered times past. A baby shoe would bring back a memory of her first steps, pictures of the three of them at her christening brought a tear to his eye. It was replaced by a chuckle when he remembered how she hated to have a bath. Such are the memories of life which we often don't take time to remember.

We were almost finished so I suggested to Mrs. Smith that she take a few days and visit her children. We would be awfully busy when we got to Oak Hill and she had not seen them since she had decided to move with us.

For the first time Bill and I found ourselves alone in the big house. It was too quiet. We had become used to the laughter from the girls rooms, the rattle of pots and pans as Mrs. Smith prepared our meals or cleaned the house. We decided, on the second day, to clean the attic together. I had been up there several times and knew that there was a lot of things from his childhood and college days as well as things that Katherine had stored. I felt that he needed to make the decisions about these things.

So off we went in our flannel shirts and jeans, coffee in a thermos and sandwiches and fruit for our lunch. We had our work cut out for us. It went really well. Most of the childhood memories would be boxed and moved to the attic in Oak Hill. Some things would be saved for Ellen to see and hear about when she was older. I still remember that a light rain had begun to fall as we spread our lunch on the attic floor and settled in a couple of old bean bag chairs. The soft sound of the rain on the roof lulled Bill into a nap. I smiled as he lay there so peaceful and relaxed. That must have been what he was like as a little boy, I thought. I tiptoed over to a corner of the attic to start unpacking another box while he slept.

The box was made of wood and had a latch on the top. A small lock had been inserted in the latch but wasn't fastened. I quietly removed the lock and lifted the lid. The rain shower suddenly turned into a storm. Lightening flashed, crackling and sparking all over the attic. It was not unusual for storms to develop suddenly in the summertime in Georgia but, for some reason I was startled and felt a sudden chill. I rolled the sleeves down on my flannel shirt and peered into the box.

There were papers which I set aside for Bill to go over. A folder with pictures of a baby in Bill's arms caught my eye. The lights were dim in this corner so I put the folder with the papers to look at later and continued to lift items from the box. If lightening had reappeared and struck me at that moment I would not have been more shocked. In the bottom of the box was a baby quilt. I lifted it out and stepped over to the window for a better look. It couldn't be! The squares were all familiar, my first Easter dress, Mother's apron...and around the edge was quilted a row of hearts; "follow your heart...follow your heart..."

I must have screamed or cried out because Bill was instantly awake and at my side. "Whatever is the matter", he said reaching to hold me close to him. I pulled back and somehow found my voice. "Where did you get this? How long has it been here?" He instantly turned white and turned his face away from me. "Where, where" I shouted again and again.

Chapter Eighteen

Without a word Bill went down the attic stairs. I followed with the quilt held tightly in my grasp. My mind was racing so fast but my steps seemed like slow motion. When I finally got downstairs I found Bill sitting at the kitchen table The storm had made it quite dark in the room but he had not turned on a light. I could see his face was still pale and there were tears streaming down his face, making a puddle on the table top.

I sat down across from him and waited for him to compose himself. Finally in a quivering voice I hardly recognized, he told me that he had always wanted to tell me a secret that he and Katherine had vowed to never tell. Somehow he had felt that she would know even after her death if he broke the promise and since it probably wouldn't matter to me he had kept it inside.

He started by telling me how much they wanted children. From the beginning of their marriage he knew that Katherine's heart wouldn't be strong enough for a pregnancy and delivery. He put her off for years by telling her how busy they were, getting him through medical school, then starting a practice. She was patient for a long time but then began to pressure him. He knew how important it was to her. They decided that they would adopt but this procedure went on and on. Several times they thought it was only days away before they would have a child, but something always happened and the months became years.

Katherine was so unhappy and her heart condition began to worsen. His love for her made him resolve to do anything in his power to get a child. He had no idea how he would accomplish this. He felt guilty that he had put her off so long. Then, as if an answer to his prayers he saw an ad in the *Atlanta Constitution.* "Motherless baby needs a home with good family."

He called the number in the advertisement and made an appointment to meet with the man who identified himself as the father of the child. He confided in Steve, his lawyer, who insisted on going with him, neither one knowing what to expect.

In a hotel room he found a young man and a month old baby girl. The man told them that his wife had died and that he could no longer care for the child. He and Steve were given a birth certificate which looked legal enough. The man wanted one hundred thousand dollars for the baby. He stated that he was leaving the country and would have no further contact with them.

Bill remembered it as if it had happened that same day. He knew that it was illegal to buy a child but all he could think of at that time was that he had to find one for Katherine. As he looked at this baby girl he knew that she could never find a better mother.

He and Steve went outside to his car where they went over the legal ramifications of such a deal. He had told Steve that he was going to give the man the money and he hoped that there would be some way they could make it legal. That was the bottom line.. this baby was going home with him.

He went to the bank, withdrew his savings and borrowed enough money to make up the hundred thousand and returned to the hotel. He would always remember that the baby's father never showed any hesitation or sadness at giving up his child. He wondered at the time what would make a father do that. He picked her up and wrapped this quilt around her and handed her over with a smile as he signed a paper Steve had hastily drawn up. He slipped the money into a guitar case that was on the bed and opened the door for them. Bill had gone over and over this episode millions of times after that but still hadn't been able to understand why the man had sold his own child. There had been times he had felt fear, but never once regret that he had done this thing.

Katherine was overjoyed when they got home and placed the child in her arms. The look on her face as she folded the quilt back and looked at her sleeping child made up for anything legal, or illegal that he had done.

The next day he and Steve had pulled some strings at the licensing bureau and had a new birth certificate made up for the baby they named Ellen.

Katherine was told how the baby was obtained and she was afraid that someday she would lose the baby. The three of them made the vow never to tell anyone. The quilt went into the attic with a little dress that she was wearing. After a couple of years her fears subsided and the manner in which Ellen became their child was never mentioned between them. Once in a while Katherine would smile and say to the little girl, "follow your heart my little Ellen", that is your legacy. Steve had taken all the paper work with him, so there was no evidence of the "sale".

"I'm sorry that I kept this from you but you must see that I had to keep my promise. What would Ellen think if she knew that I had bought her? She can't remember how much she meant to her mother, she wouldn't understand. Please promise me that this will be our secret now." Ellen loves you. You are the Mother that she has known since she was three. Can we keep it this way?" Bill implored me with shaky voice and grief stricken eyes.

Chapter Nineteen

I could not speak. I could hardly breathe. Taking the quilt I went upstairs to Ellen's empty room and locked the door. I lay on her bed for the rest of the afternoon and held the quilt, trying to understand what Bill had told me.

My Catherine didn't die in that plane crash? Kevin had brought her to Atlanta while I was making plans to bury my parents and sold her for a hundred thousand dollars? Her real Mother had died, that was his story? It was more than I could comprehend.

Bill knocked on the door several times, but I did not answer. The rain stopped during the long night. My tears began to fall just as the sun began to lighten the sky and there was no controlling them. There were tears of rage, tears of sadness and tears of joy. I let them fall on the quilt I still held in my arms. The memory of Mother and I piecing and quilting the two identical quilts seemed to bring a calmness after awhile and I knew that I was going to be OK.

I walked around Ellen's room when daylight came looking at things that I seemed to be seeing for the first time. A picture of she and Bobbie wearing their Christmas crosses. That's why Bill was questioning the birth date. Bobbie is Ellen's aunt! I am her Mother! It was too much to take in at once.

Bill came to the door with some coffee and said he was leaving for the office. He didn't understand why I was so upset but we could talk about it later. No, he didn't know why I was upset. How could he ever know that I was the Mother on the birth certificate that they replaced. How could he know that I had spent thirteen years with a hole in my heart. How could he know the nights I had prayed that I would find my baby or how many nights I had cursed God for letting her be killed in that plane crash. How many nightmares I had of her burned body on that hillside.

Who was the baby in the plane? It was probably Iris' little boy. The long-ago clipping stated that there was a woman on the plane, didn't it? It seemed so long ago that I opened the envelope to find the newspaper clipping. Who had sent it to me? Maybe someone had left the band before that fateful day and remembered me. How many of them knew what Kevin had done? Did Mary? She had told me in the beginning that the band would always come first. How right she was...

I bathed and dressed. Putting on enough makeup to cover my red eyes and puffy face and went downtown. The traffic on Peachtree was hectic as usual but I drove as if in a daze and found a parking garage next to Steve's office. His receptionist greeted me with a smile and asked if I had an appointment. I told her to tell Steve that I wanted to see him about a newspaper ad and a bill of sale.

Steve came to the door himself and invited me to come in. His face was flushed and hands shaking as he led me to a chair. "You look like you could use some coffee." he said. "No, I just need to hear a story from you", was my reply. After explaining the discovery in the attic and repeating Bill's story I asked him what he could add. "That's pretty much the whole story", he said. "I am not surprised that Bill didn't tell you before. He has lived in fear that somehow the man would come back and cause trouble, and that Ellen would find out that he was not her birth father."

Chapter Twenty

"He won't be coming back to cause trouble", I said. "He won't be coming back at all." What do you know about him that we don't?" Steve asked questioningly. I pulled the newspaper clipping from my purse and handed it to him, not taking my eyes from his face. After he read the clipping I told him that now I had a story to tell. I had not told Bill so he would be the only one to know.

He looked at me in disbelief as I told him of my life with Kevin, leaving my baby girl to go to Bobbie when our parents both died on the same night. Searching for years for some trace of Kevin and the baby and then receiving the newspaper article. I could tell that he wasn't too sure if he believed my story. It was somewhat incredible I had to admit. "Did you keep the original birth certificate?", I asked. "It's in a private file. I wanted to be sure that there wouldn't be any problems for Bill and Katherine so I kept everything here in the office" was his reply. "Look at the names on the birth certificate and you will see that I am telling you the truth," I told him. He went into another room and I heard the clicking sounds of a safe opening. When he came back into the room he had a thin folder in his hand." Her name is Catherine Elaine Ball, she was born one month before the duplicate you made. Her parents were Ann and Kevin. She was born in Oak Hill, Florida", need to know more?

Steve dropped the folder on his desk and sat down in the chair next to me. Reaching over to take my hand, he said, "This can't have happened" It is too incredible for words. That you would come to Atlanta, go to work for Bill, meet Katherine and Ellen and become Bill's wife, it is just too much of a coincidence." "Yes, it couldn't have been a coincidence," I replied. "It had to have been a answer to the thousands of times I asked God to give me my baby back. He just did it in His own time, in His own way."

As we sat there in Steve's office, letting the events of the last 24 hours sink in, I asked him if he would tell Bill my story. I didn't see how I could. I knew that he would be devastated when he learned how much grief I had been through. Even though he didn't regret what he had done, he had to know what pain it had caused me. Steve called Bill's office and requested he return his call. He would make an appointment to see him after his office hours and talk to him.

I didn't know how I would face him, but I knew that we both would need some time to get things straight in our minds and hearts. I wasn't sure if I could keep his secret forever.

Steve called about six to tell me that he had talked to Bill. He had left the office in shock. I was to call him if either of us needed anything." You'll both be OK", Steve said. "You love each other and have a lot of good years left with your girls."

I was relieved when Bill's nurse called and said he would probably be at the hospital all night. Maybe by tomorrow I would be able to face him.

I sat alone in our beautiful house. The house that Bill and Katherine had bought before the baby girl that was to be their's came. I remembered the years when we first met. Katherine was such a good mother. She had taken Bobbie and I to her heart and helped in so many ways during the hard times while I searched for the child that was right there in my apartment so many times.

Sometime during that night I made the decision to tell Bill that the secret could be ours, as it had been his and Katherine's.

When he came home the next afternoon I could tell that he had not slept, probably hadn't eaten either. I took him in my arms and with my tears joining his, told him my decision.

We lay for hours that night talking and thinking about the strange fate that had brought us together. "The funny thing is how easily Ellen came to love you, I think even before Katherine died", he said. "That is how I can live with the decision not to tell her that I am her birth mother", I replied. "I know she loves me and what good would knowing that her real father was an awful, selfish, dishonest person do. I don't think that she would love you any less. I have come to realize that by answering that newspaper ad, you kept someone else from having my baby. Maybe someone else that I would have never have known. I guess I owe you my gratitude."

The quilt was put in one of the boxes to go to the attic in Oak Hill and by the time the children returned and we made the move our shock had worn off and life resumed for the five of us.

Mrs. Smith was settled in her little house and she was never lonely. Either she was at our house helping me to make it into our home, or the girls were at her house learning to sew, cook and garden.

Bill got the research lab set up and was the happiest I had ever seen him. We had made a promise that we would never keep secrets from each other and it was nice to be able to talk to him about anything.

He loved Oak Hill and the townspeople soon grew to love him. Bobbie had decided to go to a college nearby and was home every weekend. She and Ellen spent a lot of time together, as they always had. So many times I would watch them and see Mother in both their behaviors. Why hadn't I seen that in Ellen before?

So, many of the dreams I had dreamed as a girl had come true. Here we sat on warm nights on the porch swing. Neighbors still stopped to chat and the girls met their friends for a coke at the drugstore or just sat on the steps talking. The sounds of their laughter drifting over to us was the most beautiful music. My life was as perfect as I had imagined it would be.

The years have a way of slipping by. The hope chest in the attic has been filled for another generation of young ladies. The crocheted doilies, the embroidered pillowcases, the dish towels and pretty nightgowns, just like Mother and I did for me.

Bobbie has already taken hers' to her own house. She found a wonderful man while she was in college and married in much the same way I did, in the garden out back. Bill proudly gave her away. He had never been the brother-in-law in their relationship. He was as much a father to her as to Ellen. I had found the "follow your heart" ring bearer's pillow and she was touched when I reminded her that Mother had made it.

Chapter Twenty One

I spend a lot of time these days in the attic. Granny's rocker is back up there temporarily. Bobbie and Ellen will be rocking their babies in it one day. Until then I sit and write. I look up occasionally and see through the little diamond shaped attic window Ellen and her friends playing ball in the meadow out back, or look over at the little house Mrs. Smith has transformed into her home. The neatly bordered flower beds, the crisp white curtains, the smell of freshly baked cookies make it hers alone. She has been such a comfort to us all in so many ways and continues in her pleasant, calm way to lead Bill and I into our "golden years" with her fine example.

Ellen is a happy, beautiful young lady. She has a lot of musical talent and plans to teach music at the high school when she graduates from college. She has her eye on a young veterinarian who recently graduated from Auburn University and set up a practice here. I am reminded of myself so many times by her actions and words. She makes no secret of the fact that she wants to live here in this house and share her life with someone as wonderful as her father. To have the love that we have is all she can dream. Didn't we all have our dreams?

Bill and I have put instructions in our will for Bobbie and Ellen to come here to the attic. They will find the wooden box with a small lock.As they together open the box they will find some things from their childhood. Some they will remember, a favorite doll, teddy bear, the green dresses they wore at our wedding and the tiny crosses with Bobbie and Ellen engraved. At the bottom of the box, under the baby quilt with the heart border they will find this manuscript. By reading this Ellen will discover for the first time the incredible story of our life. How we lost each other, how unbelievable circumstances brought us back together and why we had to keep the secret.

I hope she will understand the relationships, mine and Kevin's, Kevin with her, Bill and Katherine, Bill and me.. She and Bobbie...

How she feels about us all is only a guess, but I believe, with all my heart, that she will understand and be comfortable with it all. We girls have always remembered to "Follow our hearts."

Nancy Holland

ABOUT THE AUTHOR

Nancy Holland was born in North Carolina and raised in a small town in Northwest Florida, where she lives with her high school sweetheart, whom she married 47 years ago. They have two daughters and two sons and four grandchildren.

Nancy has written poems, short stories and plays for friends and family. Two poems, *They Write Their Names on My Driveway* and *For Mae* were previously published.

She was encouraged by her granddaughter to write *Follow Your Heart* based on a dream.

The illustrations were done by Carole Holland Buttrick.

Printed in the United States
2191